MAKI

CYNTHIA MERCATI

A SAMUEL FRENCH ACTING EDITION

FOUNDED 1830

SAMUELFRENCH.COM

PRODUCTION NOTE

MAKIN' IT is designed to be produced as simply or as elaborately as the director may wish. Platforms may be used to set off the three distinct playing areas; all props and scenery may be either real or imagined, depending upon budget or interpretation.

At the heart of MAKIN' IT are a number of monologues in which characters step out of the action to address their thoughts directly to the audience. At each of these "inner monologues," all other action on stage should freeze. The character speaking must become the absolute focus of attention. This may be achieved with lighting, in which case lights dim on the frozen action as the character moves away and into a spot, or by the establishing of a specific area in which the actor moves for the monologue. Either way, the actor must assume a position of strong focus. At the end of the monologues, the lights come back up on the rest of the action, and the character rejoins the scene, or exits, whatever is indicated in the script.

CAST

SCOTT BARROWS	BURNOUT
HUNTER DUNBAR	LIBBY
KARL SWANSON	JEN
BUZZARD FISHBECK	PAT
VINCE CARNELLI	BARB
ED BARROWS	SHARON
HOWIE	MONICA
TRAVIS	CORLY BARROWS
ALEX	BEV BARROWS
LEN	SYBIL DUNBAR
BROOKE BENEDICT	MRS. COZLOWE
	MS. HEALY

ANNOUNCEMENT VOICE

Sybil Dunbar and Ms. Healy may double as students.

TIME

The present

PLACE

Dwight D. Eisenhower High School

MAKIN' IT

ACT ONE

Mainstage is a student lounge, a row of lockers Center, benches Right and Left. Signs and banners advertising various school functions can be hung in the lounge.

The other two playing areas are small and require only a desk, Left, and a table and several chairs, Right. These areas may be either Down Right and Down Left of the lounge area, on the apron of the stage, or on platforms set Up Right and Up Left.

The action is continuous, one scene flowing into the next. Often the actors must take up their positions during the preceding scene to keep the action uninterrupted. JEN, HOWIE, MONICA, and ALEX are downstage, facing front, peering intently into hand-held mirrors. The dialogue is fast, sharp, almost overlapping, JEN, HOWIE, and MONICA growing increasingly anxious and up tempo, ALEX confident, cool. These roles may be taken by additional actors if a larger cast is desired.

JEN. Weird!
HOWIE. Gross!
MONICA. Desperate!
ALEX. Totally hot!
HOWIE. Look at these zits—
MONICA. —these clothes—
JEN. —this hair—
ALEX. *(Flexing)* This bod.

JEN. *(Desperately poking at her hair)* I could color it—

HOWIE. *(Desperately poking at his acne)* —use some Clearasil—

MONICA. *(Desperately grabbing and jabbing at her clothes)* —get a new skirt—

ALEX. *(Mimes dabbing it on)* A little aftershave—

JEN. —cut it — curl it—

ALEX. *(Debating, as he studies his hair, comb in hand)* —comb it?—

MONICA. —another sweater—

HOWIE. —some more Clearasil—

MONICA. —another blouse—shoes—socks—

HOWIE. —some *more* Clearasil—

ALEX. *(Putting the comb away)* —Nah.

HOWIE. My face looks like a pepperoni pizza!

MONICA. Weird!—

JEN. Millions of people in this world and I had to get this hair!

HOWIE. Gross!—

MONICA. I might as well wear a sign that says "My Mother dresses me!"

JEN. Desperate!—

OFFSTAGE VOICE. You're going to be late for—

JEN, HOWIE, MONICA. *(In varying degrees of terror and panic)* —school!

ALEX. *(With an expansive gesture, right into the mirror)* Lookin' good! *(A sharp, sudden pause, then we hear his doubt)* I hope — *(A bell rings and simultaneously, the four merge into the mainstage area as students enter from Right and Left and flood the lounge with the normal din of a high school, clustering around their lockers, several of the guys tossing a football back and forth.*

There's laughter, shouted comments about last night's date, the summer, upcoming games. JEN and BROOKE are Center, ad libbing conversation. The announcement voice breaks over the din, relentlessly cheerful)

ANNOUNCEMENT VOICE. Good morning! *(Catcalls, whistles and other derisive noises rise up in greeting)* And here are today's announcements: *(Picking up speed as she goes)* D lunch will switch with A lunch, B with C, and all lunch periods will be lengthened 15 minutes, except for A, which is now D and will be 15 minutes shorter, and B which is now C and will be 10 minutes longer, and E— *(Her favorite part, with near hysterical happiness)* which will disappear entirely!! Today's hot lunch is Tater Tot and Spam casserole over cabbage rolls! *(More derisive noises)*

BUZZARD. *(His voice rising above the others)* Burp city! *(As the students disperse, JEN and BROOKE remain Center, still settling things at their lockers, conversation continuing. JEN has a dry sense of humor with which she tries to combat life. BROOKE is vulnerable, too eager to please, with a below the surface determination she doesn't yet know she has)*

JEN. I don't see how you can just suddenly turn yourself into another person. You've spent 17 years becoming who you are.

BROOKE. *(With passion)* I've spent 17 years speaking when spoken to—making good grades—and *not* making waves. And absolutely no one knows who I am. I'm nothing—less than nothing, because even the zeroes get noticed.

JEN. *(Dryly)* You want attention? Shave your head and pull the fire alarm.

BROOKE. *(This matters—it really matters)* I want to walk

down these halls and have all the guys smile at me—I want the popular girls to ask me to their parties. I want to be *someone*.

JEN. This school is not the world!

BROOKE. It's our world.

JEN. We graduate in the spring—then we can go anywhere and be anything we want! We won't even remember the four lousy years we spent here.

BROOKE. *(With conviction)* Oh, yes, we will. Everyone remembers high school. My Mom told me. She remembers every hour of every day she spent in high school. She was a prom queen and a pompom girl—there's half a page in the yearbook just about her.

JEN. The woman peaked at 17—that leaves a lot of years for your pompoms to molt.

BROOKE. Maybe you really don't care— *(Shrewdly)* Or maybe you do and you're just covering up. But not me. Not anymore. I've got a plan—I thought about it all summer. I get off the bus looking like this, hit the john, and then— *(And from her purse she pulls a hot, slightly outrageous outfit, part of which may be concealed under her present costume for a quicker change. Defiantly she holds it up to herself)* What do you think?

JEN. I think your Mother will kill you if she finds out you're changing clothes at school.

BROOKE. Too bad. It's not like when she was young— you don't score by being the nicest or the sweetest anymore. *(With a hard edge)* If my Mother wants me to be popular, she'll have to pay the price. *(Exits Right. Taking several steps Downstage, JEN addresses the audience. All other action freezes. Lights dim, spot up on JEN. [At each "inner mono logue", all action freezes as the character steps forward. Lights dim and the character moves into a spot])*

JEN. All right, so no one knows my name—so I won't be voted cutest girl in the senior class. It doesn't matter. I'm a late bloomer. My Dad told me so. He said everyone in his family is a late bloomer. He said he didn't hit his stride until his 30's, and now look at him! Why, he's— *(And she's brought up short, realizing just what her father is—and isn't)* Well, maybe it'll be different for me. *(With bravado)* After all, I've got a plan, too—I'm going to be someone where it really counts. Out there. In the real world. I Am Woman-right? The possibilities are unlimited! I could be a soap opera actress or a game show hostess—or one of those women in the commercials, the ones with the fluffy hair and the thin thighs, who run the big corporations during the day and wear satin lingerie at night. *(A light in her eyes, she can see it all)* And then I'll hit the talk shows. There I'll be, chatting it up with Johnny and Phil and Oprah and Dave—cracking jokes in front of a hundred zillion people. And when they ask me about high school, I know just what I'll say—*(A touch of bitterness to her vigor)* "Shove it up your nose, Dwight D. Eisenhower High!" So you see, none of this really matters, because I've got plans, too. *(A certain desperation to her bravado now)* And if they don't work out—at least they get me through the day. *(Lights up. JEN exits Right as MONICA enters the lounge Right, BARB and SHARON entering Left. MONICA is one of those kids who never quite fits in—who's always on the edge—and she knows it. BARB and SHARON are the opposite, golden girls, arbiters of the social scene. Entering, they quickly surround MONICA with high powered charm and false friendliness)*

SHARON. Monica! Hi!

BARB. Going out for cheerleading this year?

MONICA. *(Bewildered at their attention)* I—I hadn't planned on it.

BARB. You should! I mean, I was in P.E. with you last year—you're really very athletic.

MONICA. *(She wants so much to believe them it's painful)* I never thought I was. I'm not— *(Dropping a book, she finishes lamely)* I'm not very coordinated.

SHARON. *(Handing her the book)* You're just being modest.

BARB. And, Monica, if you're a cheerleader—you get to go to all the good parties.

SHARON. It's a blast!

MONICA. *(Lapping it up like an eager puppy)* It would be fun.

SHARON. Well, all right then! See you at tryouts?

MONICA. Okay! *(SHARON and BARB can barely stifle their laughter as MONICA exits Left, HUNTER and PAT entering Right, hand in hand, and totally absorbed in one another. HUNTER'S cool is practiced, polished—deadly. Quickly SHARON and BARB cross to them)*

BARB. *(Conspiratorially)* Monica bought it—she's going to try out for cheerleading!

HUNTER. *(Briefly)* What a skag.

BARB. It'll be a riot!

PAT. *(There's a vulnerable side to her hard edge)* She can't chew gum and walk at the same time— Healy'll have a fit. *(BUZZARD FISHBECK, the true wild man of this school, enters Left. He wears a hat, shades, and carries a jam box, to which he's blissfully lip synching as he goes, a comic book stuck in his back pocket. A man in a world of his own)*

BUZZARD. *(As he passes them)* Lookin' good, ladies.

SHARON. *(With bite)* Wish we could say the same.

BUZZARD. Face it, baby—you want me.

SHARON. *(With vigor)* Jerk!

BUZZARD. *(Blithely)* She's just covering up. *(And he settles down on a bench for a good read)*

HUNTER. Why don't you creep back under the rock you came out of, Fishbeck?

BUZZARD. *(This doesn't faze him—nothing does)* No can do, man—I was hatched. *(COZLOWE enters the lounge Right. Firmly, grimly, she shuts off the music)*

COZLOWE. *(She's got a way with tight lipped sarcasm)* I see we can look forward to another interesting year, Mr. Fishbeck.

BUZZARD. I'll do my best.

COZLOWE. Well, what I suggest you do right now is get a new attitude! *(And she exits Right, confident the moral victory is hers)*

BUZZARD. *(Calling after her)* Couldn't I buy one used? *(TRAVIS and ALEX enter Right, ad libbing conversation, KARL following. KARL is a successful athlete, but he's more intense than the other kids, with a dark side. His manner is rough, his clothes, although clean, are old and out of date, and he knows it, and suffers embarrassment because of it. TRAVIS and ALEX are Hunter's satellites)*

HUNTER. *(His politeness is somewhat patronizing)* Going to set some new records this year, Karl? *(KARL slams his books as he stacks them in his locker, trying to cover up with a defensive attitude)*

KARL. Gotta get in the games first. The new principal

said if I don't bring up my grades, I don't play.

TRAVIS. The guy must be a real idiot!

BUZZARD. *(Without looking up from his comic book)* Relax, man, if you take enough steroids maybe your brain'll grow.

ALEX. If you don't play, we don't win—can't your old man talk to the principal? *(KARL takes a few steps Downstage to address the audience. Others freeze. KARL crosses to spot. His thoughts are dark, brooding—bitter)*

KARL. My old man. That's a laugh. The only thing he ever did for me is beat me black and blue and bust a couple ribs. And he treated the rest of the family just as swell. I used to take my brothers and sisters and hide under the bed when he started beatin' on Mom—and pray he wouldn't find us. And once in a while he'd be so drunk he wouldn't. Mom said we couldn't tell anyone. She said there were some things you just didn't let other people know. She always acted like it was her fault. It's better now, though. I'm bigger than he is and stronger—and he knows it. *(With grim relish)* I'll never forget the look on his face when I told him that if he ever laid a hand on Mom again or any of the kids—or me—I'd kill him. Plain and simple. And I would. Stupid. That's what he used to call me when he was beatin' me up. Stupid. I never could catch on to things too quick—but I sure caught on to football. There's nothin' I can't do on that field. Football's gonna be my ticket *out.* I'm gonna get a scholarship—to one of those big schools, where they put you on TV and you read your name in the paper every other day. Then I'm turnin' pro. I'll make a million bucks a year, do commercials for everything from underwear to car batteries. Yeah, football's gonna get me out. Make me someone. *(With desperate passion)* And there'll be so many people cheerin' for me—shoutin' my name—screamin' their lungs out for me, I'll *never, ever* hear the old man's voice—or feel his fists—again. *(He turns again to his locker. Cross fade up and action resumes)*

HUNTER. Remember—party at my house after the first game.

BUZZARD. Wouldn't miss it.

TRAVIS. *(Bending down, Right to Buzzard)* It's only for humans. *(And in answer, BUZZARD belches loudly and prolongedly in TRAVIS' face. Quickly, sharply, TRAVIS yanks off Buzzard's shades, and in one neat move, breaks them in two, then tosses them back)*

BUZZARD. *(Studying what's left of his shades, completely undaunted)* Gee—when you spend a buck fifty at K-Mart you expect things to last.

HUNTER. *(With that patronizing kindness)* I'd really like to see you at the party, Karl.

KARL. *(Shutting his locker, he says tersely)* Sure.

HUNTER. You'll get around this ridiculous rule.

KARL. Yeah. *(Exits the lounge, Left)*

SHARON. I know Karl is a big jock and all that, but I wonder if he's got the right clothes for a party.

HUNTER. Karl Swanson is more than just a jock, lady, he's been all-conference three years in a row. He's a legend in his own time—and it never hurts to be seen with a legend.

SHARON. You mean he's in?

HUNTER. *(With surety)* I mean he's in through football season. *(Carrying a portfolio, SCOTT enters Right. He's a good kid, a quiet kid, a kid like hundreds of others you'll find in the halls of any high school. As he attempts to open his locker, TRAVIS blocks his way, the others looking on, the girls with a kind of amused embarrassment, HUNTER and ALEX relishing every minute)*

SCOTT. That's my locker.

TRAVIS. *(With obnoxious innocence)* You're kidding? Is it really your locker? *(To the others)* Hey—this is his locker!

SCOTT. *(His protest is mild, if definite, he doesn't really want to make waves)* I'd like you to move—

TRAVIS. What?

SCOTT. *(Starting to steam, distinctly)* I'd like you to move.

TRAVIS. *(Really pushing him)* I can't hear you, man.

SCOTT. *(With real anger now)* Move it!

TRAVIS. *(The response he was waiting for, he gives him a small shove or two, daring him)* Getting tough, huh?

HUNTER. *(Belittling him with sarcastic politeness)* You're the plumber, aren't you?

SCOTT. *(Stiffly)* My Dad's a plumber, I help him out sometimes.

HUNTER. I thought so. Saw the old man's truck in front of school the other day. "Barrows Plumbing" in red and green—very festive. *(There's laughter at that)*

SCOTT. We like it.

HUNTER. You seem real jumpy, boy. You nervous about something? *(And so saying, he grabs Scott's portfolio)*

SCOTT. *(Making a try for it)* Give it back— *(But ALEX and TRAVIS move in on him, forming a united front as HUNTER leafs through the portfolio)*

HUNTER. What have we here? *(Consideringly, with mock*

seriousness) Not bad. You have some very interesting pictures here, Mr. Barrows. I think you ought to share them with the world. *(And he tosses the portfolio to TRAVIS who tosses it to ALEX, who tosses it back to HUNTER, and so on, playing a game of dodge ball, as SCOTT tries repeatedly to lunge for the portfolio)*

SCOTT. Give me back my stuff!

TRAVIS. I'm shakin'—the artist is getting tough!

ALEX. What ya gonna do? Break a paintbrush over our heads?

TRAVIS. Or maybe a plunger?

HUNTER. All right, gentlemen, enough of this horseplay. Give the boy back his possession. *(And TRAVIS shoves the portfolio hard into Scott's middle, doubling him over as HUNTER drapes a congenial arm over Scott's shoulders)* You'll have to come up to my house sometime, Barrows—it's a plumber's paradise. Lots of toilets. *(And at this there's an explosion of laughter)*

BUZZARD. *(Mildly, not looking up from his comic book)* Is that because you're so full of it, Hunter?

HUNTER. *(Distinctly)* It's because my house is the biggest one in town, jerk face.

SCOTT. *(Hurt and humiliation spilling over)* We all know you're rich, Dunbar. Big deal.

HUNTER. *(Right to him, with intensity)* You bet it's a big deal, buddy. You bet it is. *(BROOKE enters Right, Jen following, but it's a very different Brooke, wearing her new clothes, a hot hairstyle, heavy on the make-up. And her attitude, too, has changed, very up, very flirty. She crosses the lounge, smiling widely at each boy in turn, eliciting a definite response, from Scott especially, as the girls size her up appraisingly)*

BROOKE. Hi! Hi! Hi! Hi, Hunter! Like—I love that sweater, Barb! *(Exits Left)*

JEN. *(With emphasis)* Like throw up. *(Exits Right. HOWIE dashes in Left, muttering frantically. HOWIE has thick glasses, a load of books, a pocket full of pens, and a perpetually harried manner)*

HOWIE. Oh, my gosh! Where am I? And where am I going?!

TRAVIS. *(To Alex)* I think I see a freshman in need of assistance. Your locker or mine?

ALEX. Yours is cruddier. *(And ALEX and TRAVIS proceed to knock Howie's books out of his hands, hoist him up and stuff him in a locker, HOWIE in abject and vocal terror the entire time, HUNTER and the girls laughing)*

HOWIE. Oh my gosh! Oh my gosh! Oh—my— *(And from inside the locker)* gosh!! *(Still laughing, ALEX, TRAVIS, SHARON, BARB, HUNTER and PAT, his arm around her, exit Left)*

SCOTT. *(Smarting)* Thanks a lot for helping me out, Buzzard.

BUZZARD. *(Cheerfully, standing)* You know my motto, man. You can always count on me—I'll always let you down. *(And he exits Right)*

SCOTT. *(Rapping on the locker)* All clear. *(SCOTT exits. Carefully HOWIE checks in both directions before creeping out and crossing Downstage to address the audience with pitiful passion. Freeze and cross fade)*

HOWIE. This is the pits! This is the absolute worst day of my life! And my life was never that great to begin with. I was happy in junior high. I had computer-club— *Dungeons and Dragons*—my *Star Trek* re-runs. But high school— *(He shudders at the very thought)* I'm never going to fit in. I'll never be a jock. I was cut from the lacrosse team—and they were one guy short! I've never asked a girl out. *(In total and firm terror)* And I never will! If only my parents had let me go directly to Cal Tech and skip high school altogether! *(HOWIE gathers up his books and dashes out. Lights out, and in the darkness we hear a prerecorded roll call, or off stage voices calling it out)* CARNOWSKY!—Here! RADLITCH!—Here! MURPHY!—Here! CARNELLI!— *(Lights up on VINCE CARNELLI sitting on the edge of his desk, Left. VINCE is the new principal, street smart, tough, and caring)*

VINCE. Yo! *(With dry humor)* That's how I answered roll call every day. Yo. I thought it sounded tough. I thought I was tough—and maybe I was. You had to be tough in my school just to survive. *(Wryly)* It was what you'd call an "inner city" school. If you could read or write you were in the honors class. Drug pushers in every hall—you could buy anything or anyone you wanted in the boys' john. The girls' too. Fighting was our favorite school sport, but we had a pretty good football team. We weren't exactly "finesse" players, of course. Every year they'd ship us out to one of the schools in the suburbs—you know, those places with the grass and the trees instead of concrete, and the windows that aren't all broken. A lot like this school. *(Still in awe, remembering)* And the houses! Yards like parks. The only places with that many rooms on our side of town were the funeral parlors. So every year we'd go out there and beat the heck out of one of their teams. We'd be on top of the world! And then we'd come back to our four story walk-ups with the punks and the dopers and the drunks on every corner, and we wouldn't feel so great anymore. . . . Doing time. That's what we called going to school. You could do hard time or easy time— and mine was the hardest there was. There was this one kid, Mick Murphy, the biggest, meanest— oldest— guy in school, and he was itching to fight me. So one day I took him on. *(With pride)* My first punch was a beauty— the only trouble was, so was his. And his second. And his third. But I didn't give. There was blood all over my face, I couldn't see a thing— but I didn't give. His guys, my guys, everyone was screaming, he was whaling away on me— I was clawing back. And right through the whole mess comes Mr. Benteen, my math teacher. A short little guy with thick glasses, he always looked like he needed a haircut. He broke right in, grabbed Mick with one hand, me with the other— both our gangs standing there with their mouths open— and told us to cut it out. *(Still amazed)* And we did. He was tougher than both of us. So I started paying attention in class. I quit fighting and started studying— and Mr. Benteen helped me get a scholarship. *(With disbelief)* Me— Vince Carnelli, in college. Right alongside the kids with the lawns. I wanted to work in a school— I wanted to find some way to reach those kids that are just doing time. So here I am— and I'm not so sure I belong. They're testing me, you know, just like we used to test the new kids. Just like Mick Murphy. They're testing the new prinicpal to see if he'll give. I called up Mr. Benteen the other night for a little pep talk. "Be tough, Carnelli," he said. "Be tough enough to care about them." *(VINCE exits Left, the action beginning Right, at a breakfast table, the BARROWS clanking their silverware, their*

breakfast bowls, CORLY ad libbing a comment or two about pass-
ing the high fiber cereal, as SCOTT tries to sneak in Left and creep
out Right without being seen. It doesn't work)

ED. *(Without even turning)* Scott!

SCOTT. *(He's lost and he knows it, sitting down, he says*
without enthusiasm) Hi.

BEV. *(A nice lady. Urging it on him)* Have some toast.

SCOTT. *(Itching to break away, he knows he's trapped)* I'll be
late, Mom—

CORLY. *(She's bright, too bright, and mouthy, very mouthy)*
Don't you know that white bread is full of preservatives?
It puffs up in your colon like a marshmellow.

ED. *(Shooting Corly a "look". He loves his kids, but he's got alot*
to learn. With enthusiasm) I picked up some college
catalogues yesterday, Scott—they've got some real
interesting business courses.

BEV. *(Still trying, to Scott)* How about some eggs?

CORLY. Don't you realize there's enough cholesterol
in a single egg to harden your arteries for all eternity?
(CORLY gets another "look" from Ed)

SCOTT. *(Hedging)* I—I'm not real sure about business,
Dad—

ED. *(With surety)* Business majors can name their own
price, Scott. You'd be one of those guys in the 3 piece
suits—the ones that take the long lunch hours and spend
the winter in the Bahamas—

CORLY. A tourist trap.

ED. Get your MBA and you'd start at what I'm not
making yet.

CORLY. Do you really want your son to be a part of that
class of society which has built its wealth on the overbur-

dened backs of the downtrodden masses?

ED. *(At his limit)* Yes!

CORLY. *(Pleasantly)* Just asking.

SCOTT. *(Sliding discreetly to the edge of his chair)* I gotta get going—

BEV. Just some juice—

CORLY. All the nutrients have been processed out of frozen juice, you know.

BEV. *(Teeth gritted in a grim lipped smile, she says distinctly)* Well, *dear,* it's too bad we don't live in California—then you could pick us some fresh oranges right off the tree!

CORLY. You'd eat pesticides?!

ED. *(As SCOTT edges farther away)* Think about it, Scott!

SCOTT. You bet! *(And with a large sigh of relief, SCOTT breaks away and crosses Downstage to address the audience, the BARROWS remaining, eating, ED paging through the sports section. Freeze. Lights fade, spot up on Scott)*

SCOTT. I love 'em, you know, I really do. They're really okay parents—and they don't push. Well, except for this business thing. It means a lot to Dad. He sees it like our family moving up in the world or something. I think it's great he's a plumber. I'm proud of him. But all this MBA stuff— *(A shake of his head)* If I have to sit in an office for the next 100 years, trying to figure out how to sell 50 more widgets a month, I'll croak! I read once that they've got this custom in China, that if you get real lucky, like if you win the lottery or the Irish Sweepstakes or something, you're supposed to buy a bird—open the cage—and let it go. . . . What a great idea. *(SCOTT crosses the mainstage and exits Left as lights come up, The BARROWS exiting as well, as LIBBY and KARL enter the lounge Right, each carrying several books. LIBBY is a softly pretty girl, quiet, too often in her own thoughts)*

KARL. *(Gesturing to his books)* I'm afraid I'm not too good at this stuff.

LIBBY. *(Sitting, she's nervous around Karl. A little breathless and unsure of how to act)* You're doing very well. And Mr. Carnelli said that as long as you show improvement in your classes, you can keep playing.

KARL. *(He sits down next to her, LIBBY reacting, as he ponders the principal)* Carnelli. He's kinda—

LIBBY. He's very different from Mr. Tildman.

KARL. I'll say. Tildman just sorta looked the other way about my grades. Carnelli plays hard ball.

LIBBY. *(Hesitantly)* I admire what he's doing. I—I think it's the right thing. *(Lightly)* Someday you'll have to know how to do something besides play football.

KARL. *(With passion)* Not in a zillion years. Not until I'm so rich it won't matter what I do—or don't do.

LIBBY. *(Gently)* I hope it works out for you.

KARL. *(Lightly teasing)* Do you ever *go* to any of the games?

LIBBY. *(Hedging)* A few— *(And then it all comes out in a rush)* Actually, I've never missed one—and I know that last season you rushed over an average of 100 yards per game and averaged 6 sacks per game—both district records!— *(She turns sharply away, trying quickly to cover)* I mean, I didn't know exactly—I must have heard it somewhere—

KARL. *(Studying her)* You're really a different kind of girl.

LIBBY. *(Instantly stiffening)* Different? Because I happen to know a few statistics?

KARL. *(Puzzling this out)* Because you're quiet—or something. Not in class, you always know the answers, but when you're just hangin' out. You don't laugh much.

LIBBY. *(Emphatically)* I *hate* gigglers.

KARL. You know stuff the other kids don't. Like in history, you know stuff that isn't even in the book.

LIBBY. *(Biting it off)* I read.

KARL. That sounds real— *(At a loss)*

LIBBY. *(Snapping it out)* Boring, right?

KARL. *(Quickly)* No! Just—different.

LIBBY. *(On the defensive, this has struck deep)* So I'm different. I didn't plan it that way—maybe it's not even what I'd choose. But it's what I am. *(Briskly, crossing away from him)* We're done for today.

KARL. *(Awkwardly crossing away)* Got ya— *(Karl exits. Cross fade as LIBBY crosses Downstage to address the audience, spilling over with accumulated hurt)*

LIBBY. Different. That word again. *(Mimicking)* "You're so *different* from the other kids," the teachers always say. "You really *care* about Henry VIII and how many wives he had—or why Russia invaded Afghanistan." And then everyone stares at me. Even my Father says it. *(Mimicking)* "You're such a *different* kind of kid. When I was your age, I was always with my friends or shooting baskets or just goofing off. You're always up in your room reading. And what do you write in all those spiral notebooks, anyway?" He doesn't have to worry, it's nothing pornographic. Or maybe that would make him worry less—at least if I was

writing porn I'd be with it. One day a girl in class asked
me what kind of music I liked. Without thinking I said,
"Classical." She laughed so hard she turned red. Right
then I decided I'd never—*ever*—let anyone know what I
was really, *really,* thinking—or wanting—or feeling. I
could fit in if I pretended more, played the game. But I
can't seem to figure out how—or maybe it's just that I
won't. My father says I'm stubborn. *(Mimicking)* "It's
amazing. A quiet, mousy little thing like you, so stubborn." I guess that's something to be proud about. Only
the way he said it, it sounded like I was stubborn about all
the wrong things. Different. It's the ugliest word in the
English language. I hate different—so I guess I hate me.
But someday I'm going to find a city or a town or a world
where *everyone* is different—and no one cares. *(LIBBY
exits Left. Lights up. JEN, ALEX, BARB, and SHARON entering
Left as BUZZARD jams his way in Right, ghetto blaster blaring.
He's lip synching madly, or if desired, actually singing, as the
others look on. The grande finale of his brief but enthusiastic routine
finds him on his knees, looking directly up at Mrs. Cozlowe—who
is looking directly down. She snaps off the radio)*

COZLOWE. *(At her grim lipped best)* The wild man of
Dwight D. Eisenhower High.

BUZZARD. So nice of you to notice.

COZLOWE. *(Distinctly)* Mr. Fishbeck, I'm giving you a
warning—the next time you order a carry out pepperoni
pizza delivered to my class, it's an automatic suspension.
(She exits Right)

BUZZARD. *(Calling after her)* Would you have pre-
ferred sausage?

ALEX. *(To Buzzard)* Faggot!

BUZZARD. *(Cheerfully)* Alex, my man! Is it true you've been clinically brain dead since the age of 6? *(And as ALEX glares at him, or gestures, or both, BUZZARD turns on the radio full blast and jams his way out Left. HUNTER and BROOKE, hand in hand, and totally absorbed in one another—appearing very much as PAT and HUNTER did in a previous scene—enter Left)*

JEN. *(Crossing to her)* Brooke! Ready for flag practice?

BROOKE. *(Hesitating)* Well—

HUNTER. *(Briefly)* Flags are for losers. She's not interested anymore.

JEN. *(Smarting, but fighting back)* Thanks for telling me. And now I've got just one more question—who died and left you boss?

HUNTER. *(Laughing, very little and very tightly)* Funny lady. *(He takes her chin in his hand in a demeaning kind of caress)* But didn't your Mother ever tell you—funny ladies don't get dates. *(This brings a giggling response from SHARON and BARB, a snicker from ALEX, and hurt and humiliated, JEN pulls away and runs quickly out Right)*

BROOKE. *(Wincing, yet unwilling to offend him)* That was kind of mean, Hunter.

HUNTER. Forget it—forget her. *(Closing in on her)* You've got more important things to think about.

BROOKE. *(Playing right along with him)* Such as? *(PAT enters, and spotting Hunter and Brooke, hangs back, watching them)*

HUNTER. *(Suggestively)* Such as—we'll talk about it later. Ride home after school? I just hit up the old man for a new Corvette—we could cruise for awhile.

BROOKE. Sounds super.

HUNTER. *(Kissing her lightly)* Super is definitely the word for it.

PAT. *(Trying for sarcastic toughness, she confronts them)* Maybe you should have "hit up the old man" for a new telephone—since yours obviously isn't working. *(But HUNTER doesn't give her a glance, concentrating on BROOKE, who is immediately uncomfortable)*

HUNTER. I got busy.

PAT. You got busy and I got dumped!

HUNTER. *(Carelessly)* I was bored.

PAT. *(With meaning)* You weren't bored the last time we were at your house, remember? No one was home. You seemed pretty interested then—pretty excited.

HUNTER. I was faking it.

ALEX. Hey, Pat—my parents are never home! *(This brings an immediate burst of laughter from SHARON and BARB, clustered around a bench with ALEX, that is quickly—if not completely—stifled when PAT glares at them. The three turn upstage in huddled conference, gossiping and occasionally shooting an interested glance at the others)*

HUNTER. *(Lightly caressing Brooke)* Later.

BROOKE. *(Uncomfortably aware of Pat and trying not be)* Later. *(HUNTER exits Left)*

PAT. *(Fighting for superiority, cool)* You're looking really good these days, Brooke.

BROOKE. *(Defensively)* Just some new clothes.

PAT. And hair and make-up. Everyone's talking about it. *(With meaning)* And *you.*

BROOKE. *(Fighting back)* Listen, Pat—I'm sorry if Hunter hurt you. But I didn't have anything to do with it.

PAT. *(Bitterly)* You bet you didn't. Hunter does the

choosing—*and* the dropping. And when he's through with you, he's through—no fuss, no muss. *(Trying for that saving toughness)* But I can take it. It's you I'm worried about.

BROOKE. *(Stiffly)* Don't be.

PAT. Don't kid yourself. *(Shrewdly)* And don't think you can use Hunter—because he does the using. *(With meaning)* I just hope you can give him what he wants. *(PAT exits Right as TRAVIS shoves the hapless HOWIE in Right, SCOTT following, SHARON, BARB, and ALEX reacting with "what a wimp"—type snickers)*

TRAVIS. Freshman alert! *(And as once again ALEX and TRAVIS stuff Howie into the locker, we hear his plaintive cries)*

HOWIE. Oh my gosh! Oh my gosh! This wasn't covered in the student— *(And from inside, pitifully, flatly)* handbook.

SCOTT. Why don't you let up on the kid, he's scared to death.

TRAVIS. It's the painting plumber.

ALEX. I thought I smelled something.

TRAVIS. *(To Scott, forcefully)* Butt in one more time, buddy—and you're history. *(The lights fade and TRAVIS moves out of the scene and Downstage to address the audience, the Action freezing behind him. Totally without apology)* I've been a bully since the first grade—I used to knock down the kindergarteners and steal their lunch money. Not that I needed the dough—I guess I needed the attention. It's always been that way. Some guys like to kick a ball up and down a field, other guys study all the time. Well, I'm not smart enough to get on the honor roll and I've never won a trophy. I never will. But when I'm shoving someone around—I don't feel so empty inside. When I'm beating on some poor slob, I really feel like someone! *(The truth)* Well—at least I don't feel like nothing. . . . *(TRAVIS turns and exits, ALEX following. SHARON and BARB crossing to a locker)*

SCOTT. *(Rapping on the locker, dryly)* Red alert is over. *(HOWIE pokes his head out)* Do me a favor and get a squirt gun or something, okay? You can't walk around these halls unarmed.

HOWIE. *(Looking wildly around)* These halls? I'm not supposed to be in *these* halls! I'm in the wrong hall in the wrong building for the wrong class at the wrong time! *(And he dashes madly out, muttering as he goes)* Oh my gosh!— Oh—my—gosh!— *(SHARON and BARB are reapplying make-up, brushing their hair, and covertly watching Scott and Brooke, nudging one another, whispering a comment or two)*

BROOKE. That was nice of you.

SCOTT. *(He noticed her before, and now we can definitely feel his attraction)* I didn't do much.

BROOKE. You tried—you stood up for someone who needed help. I—I admire that.

SCOTT. *(Wryly)* Yeah, I'm a regular Robin Hood. *(And she smiles at that, SCOTT smiling back)*

BARB. *(Calling out, still at her locker)* Hey, Brooke—sit at our lunch table today, okay?

BROOKE. *(She's made it and she knows it, happily)* Great!

SCOTT. Brooke Benedict, right?

BROOKE. *(Her attention immediately back on Scott, throughout this scene, BROOKE is torn)* Scott Barrows, right?

SCOTT. You're in my English class.

BROOKE. I know.

SCOTT. *(In total amazement—and joy)* You do?

SHARON. *(Calling it out)* Maybe we can hit the mall tonight, Brooke.

BROOKE. Sure! *(Back to Scott)* I saw you working on a painting in the art room.

SCOTT. *(Embarrassed)* That.

BROOKE. What's it a picture of?

SCOTT. *(Hedging)* Nothing really, just colors—feelings—

BROOKE. I liked it.

SCOTT. *(Inordinately pleased)* You did?! *(Quickly, trying for cool)* It's nothing. *(Putting the final touches on hair and make-up, SHARON and BARB close in on Brooke, effectively shutting out Scott)*

SHARON. I could die for that skirt, Brooke.

SCOTT. *(Taking a few steps, lingering)* I'd better get going—

BARB. Don't let Pat get you down, she's lost her man and she knows it.

BROOKE. *(Eyes on Scott)* See ya—

SHARON. Hunter is too cute.

BROOKE. He's not bad—

SCOTT. *(Still leaving, still lingering)* In English—

BARB. Not bad?! He's got the face and the bod!

SHARON. And the bucks!

BROOKE. *(Calling to him)* In English— *(And SCOTT exits, giving BROOKE a last smile as he goes)*

BARB. What are you wasting your time with that zero for?

SHARON. His clothes are from nowhere and he doesn't even have a car. *(Nudging Barb as MONICA enters and heads for her locker, whispering)* Here she comes.

BARB. *(With overdue sincerity)* Sorry you didn't make cheerleading, Monica.

SHARON. Yeah. That was really tough. But there's always pompoms. *(At this, they can't supress a giggle)*

MONICA. *(She's hurt, yet with dignity)* I'm through trying out for things—you'll have to get your laughs somewhere else. *(And she exits)*

BARB. *(Calling after her)* Don't feel too bad—maybe someone'll nominate you for prom queen! *(Laughing, BARB and SHARON cross Downstage, addressing the audience, but not each other, in a kind of point/counterpoint dialogue. Freeze, cross fade)*

BARB. *(Flippant)* The other kids taught me all there is to know about being mean—that's why I'm so good at it.

SHARON. *(Rather maliciously)* She was the fattest girl in the first grade.

BARB. And every grade thereafter.

SHARON. *(With vicious emphasis, as a child might say it)* Chunk-o. Chubb-o. Lard butt. Jelly roll. Jelly donut.

BARB. *(And now the pain starts to seep out)* I couldn't run. Couldn't jump. My clothes were always too tight. I didn't have any friends—but I had food. Even the teachers treated me like crud. Oh, they'd probably say they didn't—maybe some of them didn't even know they were doing it. *(Bitterly)* But they were. One of 'em even asked me in front of the whole class if my parents were fat. She said I might have "genetic" problems.

SHARON. Chunk-o. Chubb-o. Lard butt. Jelly roll. Jelly donut.

BARB. One time after school the kids got me on the teeter totter, and then a whole bunch of 'em climbed on the other end—they kept me up in the air for an hour calling me names, daring me to jump down. But I couldn't. . . . I was too scared—and too fat. When they ran away I sat on the ground and cried—and ate my squished Snickers bar.

SHARON. Chunk-o. Chubb-o. Lard butt. Jelly roll. Jelly donut.

BARB. When I was about ten, my Mom told me she wouldn't take me to the Mother/Daughter banquet at church. She said I was big and fat and sloppy and she was too embarrassed to be seen with me. I just sat there. All night. Didn't even blink. Mom cried and cried and said she loved me, said that she didn't mean any of it-she was just so desperate for me to lose weight. I said I believed her. And I did . . . I guess. But way down deep inside there's a tiny little place that isn't so sure. When I got thin she bought me a whole bunch of new clothes—told me to forget all about that old me, that she didn't exist anymore. The only trouble is, whenever I look in the mirror—it's old jelly donut looking back.

SHARON. *(Very bright, very brittle)* I never worry about my weight. Not anymore. See, I've got this wonderful trick. Whenever I pig out, which is about once a day, I just head for the john and make myself throw up. Simple, huh? *(Lights up as SHARON and BARB cross Upstage and exit the lounge Right, and BROOKE exits Left, calling out to her)*

BARB. Don't forget lunch! *(LIBBY and KARL enter the small playing area Left)*

LIBBY. You should be proud of yourself, Karl—your

grades are up in every subject.

KARL. *(Awkwardly)* So how 'bout lettin' me make it up to you? For all you hard work, I mean. Wanna get somethin' to eat after I meet with Carnelli?

LIBBY. *(Stiffly, defensively)* You don't have to "make anything up" to me.

KARL. That's not what I meant—

LIBBY. That's what you said. *(And quickly she brushes past Vince, entering Left, saying briefly)* Hello, Mr. Carnelli. *(Exits)*

CARNELLI. Libby. *(Indicating the papers he holds)* I've been looking at your recent test scores, Karl. You've been working. Hard.

KARL. *(Tersely)* I've got to play.

CARNELLI. *(Mildly)* Not you'd *like* to—you *want* to? You've *got* to?

KARL. *(With tight emotion)* Football's my one way ticket outta here and away from— *(He catches himself, stopping short)*

VINCE. *(Gently)* Away from what goes on at home?

KARL. *(Angrily)* Someone's been talkin' to you.

VINCE. Or maybe I talked to someone—or saw something—or just figured out a few things on my own. It doesn't matter. What matters is that *you* talk to someone. Deal with it.

KARL. I do. In my own way.

VINCE. Out on the football field?

KARL. Maybe.

VINCE. *(Gently)* What happens when the games end?

KARL. *(With clenched emotion)* They never will.

VINCE. *(A slight pause, we see VINCE considering how to con-*

tinue, and then—) Your doctor was here today.

KARL. *(Lashing out)* He had no business comin' here! He said it was my decision—so did the coach!

VINCE. It still is your decision.

KARL. And I've already made it. I play.

VINCE. And take the chance that you might rack up your knees so badly, you'll never play college ball?

KARL. *(Desperately)* If I don't play now—if the scouts don't see me—I'll never *get* to college!

VINCE. There are other ways to get to college.

KARL. *(His sarcasm born out of pain)* Sure. Maybe I'll get an academic scholarship—and then my PhD.

VINCE. *(Gently)* Anything's possible. I know.

KARL. And I know that I've always been the fastest kid on the block and the strongest—and the dumbest. Just ask my Dad. Take football away—and I'm nothin'. *(Quickly, angrily, KARL exits, as the action begins Right, at the Barrows home, ED, BEV, and CORLY once again passing plates, munching and crunching, as once again SCOTT tries to creep in and out unnoticed—failing miserably)*

ED. *(Without turning around—he has radar)* Scott!

SCOTT. *(With that same flat enthusiasm, sitting)* Hi.

BEV. *(Urging it on him)* Have some lunch.

SCOTT. I already ate.

CORLY. And I suppose you included something from each of your four favorite food groups—Ho-Ho's, Ding-Dongs, Scooter Pies, and Twinkies?

SCOTT. You have a smart mouth.

CORLY. *(Pleasantly)* Better than clogged arteries.

ED. *(With heavy enthusiasm)* So—what did you think of those college catalogues? Great business courses, huh?

SCOTT. *(He knew this was coming)* I—really didn't have time to look at 'em, Dad.

ED. *(A slow burn)* You have time to work at that paint store.

BEV. *(Patiently)* An art store. It's an *art* store, Ed. *(Proudly)* Scott helped me pick out a Gauguin print there the other day.

CORLY. *(Brightly)* Did you know that Gauguin ditched his wife and lived on a tropical island with women who didn't wear tops?

ED. *(He's reached his limit—yet again)* That does it—no more Masterpiece Theatre for her!

CORLY. Doomed to a life of cartoon violence.

SCOTT. *(Wincing, but he's got to say it)* About college, Dad—I know it means a lot to you, since I'd be the first one from the family to go and all that, but—

BEV. Your Father went to college—he just didn't finish.

SCOTT. *(Very surprised)* Oh, yeah?

ED. *(Making light of it)* I wanted to, but my Dad had other plans—like me taking over his work. I didn't mind.

BEV. *(Gently)* You minded.

ED. *(Tersely)* That was a long time ago. It's Scott's turn now and he's got to pick a college—and soon—so he can get in the one he wants.

CORLY. *(Knowingly)* What Scott wants is Brooke Benedict.

SCOTT. *(Furious—and embarrassed)* You shut up—you little rug rat!

CORLY. *(Pleàse at his response)* Do I perceive we're somewhat sensitive on this particular subject?

ED. *(Waving his fork first at Scott)* You watch your language— *(And then at Corly)* And you stop talking like someone on the BBC!

CORLY. *(Sweetly)* Have some broccoli, Dad—you could use the roughage.

ED. Gauguin! Roughage! What do you think this is— San Francisco?!

CORLY. *(Completely unfazed, still on her own tangent)* Of course, if Scott ever *got* Brooke Benedict, he probably wouldn't know what to do with her—philosophically speaking.

SCOTT. *(With gritted teeth)* Philosophically speaking— how do you know about her anyway?!

CORLY. I saw her name written all over your notebook. *(Proudly)* and when I found that painting of a girl in your room, I deduced it must be her. She.

SCOTT. *(Boiling over)* You were in my room!

CORLY. Mind like a steel trap.

SCOTT. *(Appealing to Bev)* She was in my room!

BEV. Is this girl a friend of yours from school, Scott?

SCOTT. *(Appealing to Ed)* She was in my room!

CORLY. *(Brightly)* If I had my own personal computer I could vent my intellectual curiosity on that, instead of sneaking into other people's rooms and degrading myself by pawing through their personal possessions.

SCOTT. *(Standing up, near hysteria)* She was in my room!!

ED. *(Waving the fork again, first at Scott)* You sit down— *(Next at Corly)* And you stay out of your brother's room— or I will tan your intellectual curiosity!

CORLY. *(Totally undaunted)* We always reduce things to such a simplistic level in this house. *(Action freezes as CORLY stands and steps Downstage to address the audience)* When I was going through the parent's drawers the other day—so sue me, I'm a snoop—I found some pictures of them when they were young. She had on love beads, a leather vest, and a fringed skirt—she looked like some kind of crazy urban Indian. The father had long hair and pink bellbottoms and a headband that said "Make love not war." Can you imagine what would happen if I said that at the dinner table some night? "Please pass the beets, and by the way—make love not war."! Total meltdown! The parents must have been really outrageous before their arteries hardened. Now the highlight of their lives is the PTA Carnival. It just shows what having kids will do to you. *(And she sits down again. Action up)*

BEV. Why don't you ask this girl over some night, Scott?

CORLY. A fox like that with the brother from another planet?

SCOTT. Mom, she barely knows I'm alive.

BEV. *(Spoken like a true mother)* That's because you don't speak up enough—you're a nice boy with some very good qualities.

SCOTT. Mom—good and nice are the kiss of death in today's American high school.

BEV. Don't put yourself down.

SCOTT. I don't have to. *(Standing)* Life is doing a pretty good job of it all by itself! *(SCOTT crosses Down Right, LIBBY at Down Left, both of them addressing the audience, but not each other, in a point/counterpoint of longing)*

Libby. Do you know how it feels to like someone so much, you can't stop thinking about him—

Scott. —her?

Libby. And how when you see him—

Scott. —her—

Libby. —it feels like there's a great big bunch of hyperactive butterflies in the pit of your stomach?

Scott. You watch her—

Libby. —him—

Scott. —walk down the hall.

Libby. You watch him—

Scott. —her—

Libby. —in the lunchroom. You watch him—

Scott. —her—

Libby. —in class.

Scott. Every one of those stupid love songs on your parent's radio station sounds just like you.

Libby. You dream about him at night—

Scott. You dream about her during the day.

Libby. And when you finally get the chance to be close to him—

Scott. To talk to her—

Libby. You're so embarrassed, you're sure he knows exactly how you feel.

Scott. You can't say a word—

Libby. Or you say the wrong words—

Scott. Or too many words.

Libby. Or you blush. I *hate* to blush.

Scott. And the worst thing of all is knowing—

Libby. He'll—

SCOTT. She'll—

LIBBY. Never—

SCOTT. Ever—

SCOTT, LIBBY. Like you back. *(SCOTT and LIBBY cross Upstage and into the lounge, as once again the mainstage is filled with noisy, jostling students. The girls laughing, talking, brushing their hair, the guys shouting, shoving, the announcement voice breaking over the din with deadly cheeriness)*

ANNOUNCEMENT VOICE. Good morning everyone! *(Catcalls)* And here are today's announcements: *(Picking up speed as she goes)* All classes will be shortened 10 minutes except 3rd and 4th hours which will be lengthened 15 minutes, and 2nd and 5th hours which will be shortened 20 minutes, and 1st hour which will become 6th hour— *(Her very favorite part)* thereby disappearing entirely!! Today's hot lunch is: Tuna and lima bean casserole, Spinach surprise and happy little jello squares!! *(A volley of protest noises)*

BUZZARD. A Rolaid riot! *(The bell rings and the lounge clears, leaving HOWIE fumbling frantically at his locker, ALEX and TRAVIS leaning one on either side of him)*

HOWIE. *(He moves a step, then stands stock still, suddenly aware of who is surrounding him)* Oh—my—

TRAVIS. Relax, kid.

HOWIE. —gosh.

ALEX. We're not gonna touch you.

TRAVIS. As a matter of fact— *(Pulling them from his pocket, he stuffs a cigarette in Howie's mouth, a beer can in his hand)* we'd like you to accept a few little tokens of our esteem. *(At this inopportune—but planned—moment, HEALY, a Phys. Ed. teacher, enters Left. TRAVIS and ALEX move quickly behind*

*her, silently breaking up, HOWIE standing there in wide-eyed
and frozen horror, a lamb led to the slaughter)*

HEALY. *(In total disgust)* I thought I'd seen everything in
these halls.

TRAVIS. *(With heavy solemnity)* Shocking, isn't it?

HEALY. *(HOWIE doesn't move a muscle as first she yanks out
the cigarette)* You're going to ruin your health— *(She grabs
the beer can)* Kill your brain cells—and spend a lot of time
in detention, Mister! *(Crossing Right, grimly)* Follow me.
*(But HOWIE remains rooted, eyes wide, mouth open, as TRAVIS
and ALEX convulse in laughter)*

ALEX. Tough break, nerd. *(Still laughing, ALEX and
TRAVIS exit Right, as BUZZARD enters Left, observing
them)*

BUZZARD. *(Waving one hand in front of Howie's frozen face)*
Kirk to Spock — come in, Spock...

HOWIE. *(Wailing)* I got detention! *(The wail becomes a
moan)* I think I'm going to be sick—or die—which-
ever's quicker!

BUZZARD. *(Bluntly)* You asked for it, space cadet.

HOWIE. *(So earnest it's pitiful)* I never ask for anything—
not even double mashed potatoes in the lunch line!

BUZZARD. That, my man, is your problem. *(Gesturing
Right)* Those guys are like wild animals—they only attack
if they smell fear. And the way you hustle around these
halls is a dead giveaway.

HOWIE. I'm conscientious!

BUZZARD. You're the roadrunner. We've gotta lighten
you up—mellow you out— *(And so saying, he yanks out
Howie's pen protector and flips it over his own shoulder)* First we

ditch the pens— *(Ditto with the tie)* Then the tie— *(As he pulls off Howie's glasses and pockets them)* and definitely the coke bottles.

HOWIE. *(Squinting profoundly)* I can't see!

BUZZARD. Great! It'll help your image. *(COZLOWE and CARNELLI enter Left. Like dry ice, she's steaming with outrage)*

COZLOWE. I've been looking for you, Mr. Fishbeck.

BUZZARD. And I thought you didn't care.

COZLOWE. *(To Vince, burning)* You see? He has an attitude problem! Not only is his behavior inappropriate, it's— *(Casting about)* un-American!

BUZZARD. *(Blithely)* So I'am an alien—deport me.

COZLOWE. But today was the last straw! He was required to hand in a report on the Revolutionary War— you do recall my words on that subject, Mr. Fishbeck?

BUZZARD. Recall 'em? I tattooed 'em on my chest!

VINCE. *(Dryly, referring to the remark)* That was unnecessary.

BUZZARD. Unnecessary? *(Rubbing his chest, with high drama)* It was downright painful!

COZLOWE. *(Biting it off)* His report was not in a blue folder. His address was not clearly marked on the cover. *(The grand finale)* And the lines enclosing the map of the battle of Bunker Hill were not straight!

VINCE. *(He wants to get this right)* No blue folder. No address. No straight lines.

COZLOWE. *(Feeling thoroughly vindicated)* Correct.

BUZZARD. *(Like an old movie con)* What is it, warden— the chair?

VINCE. *(Mildly)* What was in the report itself?

COZLOWE. I have no idea. *(With dignity)* I will not read any report that is incorrectly prepared.

VINCE. That's your prerogative.

COZLOWE. That's my rule. *(Distinctly)* I'm not just teaching my students history, Mr. Carnelli—I'm attempting to teach them the importance of learning to obey the rules! *(Suddenly suspicious)* You do believe in learning to obey the rules, Mr. Carnelli?

VINCE. If they're good rules.

COZLOWE. They're *my* rules. And they've been my rules for over 30 years! And I want you to know, Mr. Fishbeck, that if you persist in breaking *my rules*—I will break *your spirit!* *(Proudly)* Conformity. Fitting in. Those are the things that count in my class, just as in life.

VINCE. *(Wryly)* Shakespeare would have had a difficult time in your class.

COZLOWE. *(With dignity)* I beg your pardon?

VINCE. *(Gently)* "To thine own self be true."

COZLOWE. *(Stiffly)* I can only hope you meant that humorously. *(And she exits Left)*

BUZZARD. *(To Vince, in amazement)* You stood up for me—no one's ever stood up for me before. Why'd you do it—when I'm such a royal pain in the butt?

VINCE. *(Mildly, yet with distinct meaning)* Just maybe—I didn't want to see your spirit broken. *(To the groping Howie, concerned)* Are you all right?

HOWIE. It's an image problem.

VINCE. *(Dryly)* I don't think the school nurse has anything for that. *(He turns to go, then turns back)* By the way, Fishbeck, your general mouthiness to Mrs. Cozlowe earned you a detention.

BUZZARD. *(Plaintively)* Has it ever occured to anyone that I might be a victim of multiple personalities? And that's it a whole other me who lips off?

VINCE. Not even remotely. *(Exits Left)*

BUZZARD. *(Taking HOWIE by the shoulder, he turns him)* Come on, kid, I'll show you the way to the slammer.

HOWIE. *(Hopefully)* Can I have my glasses back then?

BUZZARD. Where we're going—you don't want to see. *(BUZZARD leads HOWIE off Right, KARL and LIBBY entering Left)*

LIBBY. I—I thought we could get together during free period— *(Fearing he might have misunderstood, she continues in an embarrassed rush)* I mean, I thought we could *study* during free period—I mean because of the econ quiz—

KARL. *(Lightly, his manner teasing)* All right, let's study during free period. Where?

LIBBY. The library?

KARL. Too stuffy. The park?

LIBBY. I can't think there.

KARL. And what does a girl like you think about anyway? *(Gently teasing)* Adverbs? Adjectives? *(Moving close, LIBBY reacting)* Football stats? *(With meaning)* Does a girl like you ever think about—football players?

LIBBY. *(Breathlessly)* I—might—

KARL. *(Pleased)* You're blushing!

LIBBY. *(Mortified)* I'm not!

KARL. It's kinda cute—I didn't know girls blushed anymore.

LIBBY. *(Moving away from him, stiffly)* I guess most girls don't.

KARL. *(Taking her by the arm or shoulder, gently drawing her back)* Don't get so uptight.

LIBBY. *(Ruefully)* Uptight. That's a good word for me. *(Almost more to herself than KARL)* My Father always says I'm too serious. Maybe it's because I'm an only child. You know—I was alone a lot, always playing make-believe. Always dreaming—

KARL. *(Awkwardly, unable to express himself)* Oh—yeah?

LIBBY. *(Snapping quickly out of her thoughts, the sharp sarcasm at her own expense)* I'm sure this is just what you wanted to talk about—my life story.

KARL. *(He means it)* It's okay.

LIBBY. *(Lashing out)* It's *not* okay! I should be trying to make you laugh—flirting with you—doing and saying all those silly things the other girls were born knowing how to say and do and that I haven't got a clue about!

KARL. *(Earnestly)* Forget it—just forget all that stuff! You'll be at the game tonight, won't you? Let's go out after.

LIBBY. Why would you want to go out with me? I've seen you with the popular kids.

KARL. What does that have to do with anything?

LIBBY. *(Bitterly, biting if off)* You said it yourself—I'm different.

KARL. *(Backing off, almost angrily)* All right—you convinced me. I'll see you at the library. It's probably a better idea anyway—no chance to goof off. *(KARL exits Left, LIBBY looking after him, as PAT enters Left, glancing back at Karl)*

PAT. *(Knowingly, to Libby)* A hunk and a half, isn't he?

LIBBY. *(Evasively)* He's nice.

PAT. Nice?! I bet he's an animal.

LIBBY. *(Trying to move around her)* Excuse me—

PAT. *(With genuine feeling)* Libby, I like you. You're smart, but you're not a know-it-all. So here's some free advice. Relax a little—have some fun. If you like Karl—go for it.

LIBBY. *(Passionately)* I don't know how!

PAT. Sure you do. All you need is something to get you going. You'd be surprised how loose you can get after a few beers. *(LIBBY and PAT exit Right as HUNTER and BROOKE enter Left)*

HUNTER. *(Backing her up against a locker, intimately)* You give off all the right vibes, Brooke. *(Deliberately)* Yeah—you *look* and *talk* a pretty good show.

BROOKE. *(Startled, maybe even a little afraid)* What?

HUNTER. *(Brutally)* But when we really get down to it—you don't.

BROOKE. *(Trying to break away)* I don't want to talk about this— *(He catches her back as SCOTT enters Left and stands back, watching them)*

HUNTER. Well, I do. *(With clear, hard meaning)* If you think you can keep on partying with my friends, riding in my car—using me to be "Little Miss Popularity"—and not give me anything back, you're dead wrong.

SCOTT. *(Quickly, angrily, crossing to Hunter, pulling his arm away from Brooke)* And you're outta line.

HUNTER. *(Sharply shrugging him off)* Bug off. This is between me and my lady.

SCOTT. *(Trying to pull her away)* You don't have to take this from him—

BROOKE. *(Confused and ashamed, she draws away from him)*
Just go away, Scott, will you—just go away and leave
me alone.

HUNTER. *(Taking her arm possessively)* You see? The
lady's made her decision. Now beat it.

SCOTT. Not until you take your hands off her.

HUNTER. Why? You want her? Sorry to disappoint
you, but she's not that much fun. Not yet. *(With a kind of
demeaning caress)* But she's going to do better, aren't you,
babe? *(At this, SCOTT grabs HUNTER with both hands and
shoves him up against a locker—just a HEALY enters Right)*

SCOTT. You creep!— *(HEALY takes firm, quick control)*

HEALY. Scott! Back off! You know fighting's an
automatic detention. *(SCOTT moves reluctantly away, still
with an eye on Hunter)*

HEALY. Brooke—you have class. *(BROOKE moves back a
step or two, knowing she should leave, but unable to. To Hunter)*
And as for you— *(She indicates Left)* I think we'd better
have a little talk.

HUNTER. *(Impatiently, with venom)* Why don't you run a
few laps, lady? Or go shave your legs—they could use
it.

HEALY. *(Angry, but still in control, she takes his arm)* Come
on, Dunbar—Mr. Carnelli's going to get in on this
one.

HUNTER. *(His vaunted cool gone, he shoves her away)* Don't
give me orders!

HEALY. *(Snapping it out)* Consider yourself suspended,
Mr. Dunbar! Get out of this school—now! *(There's a pause
as he faces them all down for a beat or two, then—)*

HUNTER. Sure. I could use a day or two away from this

hole. *(To Scott, with emphasis)* Just remember, Barrows—
you're nothing around here. Nobody. *No one. (And he
follows Healy out Left)*

SCOTT. Why do you let him treat you like that?

BROOKE. *(Struggling to explain, anguished)* I want so much
to matter—I want to be *wanted.* Hunter—He gives me
that.

SCOTT. No one can give that to another person—you
give that to yourself.

BROOKE. *(Lashing out, her cruelty born out of hurt and
humiliation)* You wouldn't understand! It's just like he
said—you're a nothing! A *nobody!*

SCOTT. *(A slight pause, then wryly)* Maybe you're right—
maybe that's exactly what I am and it's just sinking in
now. *(He starts toward the small playing area Right, now detention, BROOKE crossing quickly after him a few steps, her words
stopping him)*

BROOKE. *(With a confusion of emotions, anger, sorrow, shame)*
I'm sorry—you tried to help me—and now you're in
trouble—

SCOTT. *(Dryly)* Yeah, well—I've always been dumb. It's
one of my "nicer" qualities. Just ask my Mom. *(SCOTT
enters detention and stands there, staring in obvious disbelief at
BUZZARD, his eyes shut as he silently lip synchs, rapping out a
song known only—heard only—by himself, HOWIE, with his
head in his hands, LEN, a freaked out punk on his own frequency
and in his own world, and BURNOUT, LEN'S female
counterpart)*

BURNOUT. Welcome to detention—or as we like to
think of it, our little home away from home.

LEN. *(With weird drama)* "Abandon hope all ye who

enter here." *(And in still silent disbelief, SCOTT sits, the action continuing in detention as BROOKE steps Downstage to address the audience. Freeze. Cross fade)*

BROOKE. *(Dreamily)* You know those girls on the cover of *Seventeen?* That's what I always wanted to look like. Perfect bodies. Perfect hair. Perfect skin. Perfect clothes. Perfect. And they make it look so easy. *(Bitterly)* But it's not. *(Tempo increasing with her frantic anger)* Always wearing the right thing—always looking just right—always saying the right thing—You can't be too loud, then you're a geek. You can't be too quiet, then you're a nerd. You can't drag home a lot of books, because then you're a grind. But if you fail, you're a burnout!— *(She stops short, collecting herself)* There's so much to remember, it makes my head ache. *(Definatly)* But it's worth it. Everyone knows me now! I party with the cool kids, sit with the cool kids, talk and walk and act just like one of them. And if I'm not . . . one of them . . . everybody thinks I am, and that's the important thing. Even my Mom. I hear her on the phone now, bragging to her friends. "Oh, Marge, the way Brooke goes out these days! The phone is always ringing—she's always out somewhere. She's one popular girl—just like I was!" But I'm not just like she was! It was easy for her . . Or maybe it wasn't. Sometimes I wish my Mom knew about the clothes and the hair and the make-up, because then I could talk to her. And sometimes I don't think she'd care if she knew, because she'd think it was worth it, too. *(Desperately)* Because it is. It's got to be. I sit with the right kids at the right lunch table and I see everyone walk by and look at us—and pretend not to look—and I know just what they're thinking. "Why can't

I do that? Be like that? Why can't I bring it off? It looks so easy." But it's not. Changing yourself, turning yourself inside out and upside down—trying to please a zillion people and make them like you—it's hard. *Seventeen* lied. It's not easy at all . . . . *(JEN enters, addressing the audience, in a point/counterpoint dialogue with Brooke)*

JEN. I told her—I told her she couldn't do it. I told her it doesn't matter who you hang out with or how you talk or look—you can't change what's inside.

BROOKE. People don't care about what's inside. Inside doesn't matter.

JEN. Inside's all that matters! The way I look at it, everything I've got is either gonna drop, droop, drag, wrinkle up, or go gray—I *gotta* work on the inside. *(The rest of the cast enters, some clustering in groups, others standing alone, sitting, kneeling, or even lying down, VINCE in his office, those Right a part of the stage picture as well. With the words that began the play—* WEIRD! GROSS! DESPERATE!—*A chant begins, it runs for a beat or two and then the dialogue resumes, addressed to the audience, not to each other, for we're hearing throughts, the chant running underneath, low and continuous)*

BROOKE. *(Dreamily)* Seventeen. I want to be the girl on the cover of *Seventeen.*

LIBBY, JEN, SHARON, PAT, BARB, MONICA. Who doesn't?

BEV. *(Sweetly)* I always wanted to be on the cover of *Ladies Home Journal,* along with my 10 secrets for a happy marriage, happy children— *(Flatly)* And tight buns.

HOWIE. *(Lifting his head to say brightly)* Computer Monthly!

LEN, BURNOUT. Shut up! *(And Howie's head descends again)*

CORLY. *(Consideringly) Newsweek?*

KARL. *(With passion) Sports Illustrated*—12 weeks running!

TRAVIS, ALEX. *Playgirl!*

SHARON. *Playboy!*

CORLY. *(Still considering) U.S. News And World Report?*

LIBBY. *Teen Scene—Teen Queen—Teen Dream*—but never—*ever*—*Poetry Journal!*

CORLY. *Atlantic Monthly?*

COZLOWE. *(Dreamily)* A *Harlequin* Romance.

HEALY. *(Assertively) MS!*

VINCE. *Boxing!*

CORLY. Maybe *Time? (Firmly)* Definitely *Time!* I could be Person of the Year! *(Amending this, smugly)* Person of the Next *Couple* of Years!

ED. *Business Weekly. Money. Financial Times. Fortune. (Then a big, sly smile, he snaps it out with dapper charm) Gentleman's Quarterly!*

HOWIE. *(His head goes up yet again, hopefully) Mad?*

LEN. *(Consideringly, to Burnout) Mad?*

BURNOUT. *(Nodding) Mad.*

LEN, BURNOUT, HOWIE. *Mad!*

BUZZARD. *Rollin' Stone! (The chant is shouted out now—* **WEIRD! GROSS! DESPERATE!**—*then once again it softens, lowers, to run beneath the dialogue)*

SEVERAL VOICES. Totally—

SEVERAL VOICES. Weird!—

SEVERAL VOICES. Totally—

SEVERAL VOICES. Gross!—

SEVERAL VOICES. Totally—

SEVERAL VOICES. Desperate!—

SEVERAL VOICES. Totally—totally—totally

SEVERAL VOICES. *(Pleading) Something!*

BROOKE. *Seventeen* lied. The hardest thing in the world is not being yourself.

SCOTT. Unless— *(The chant ends abruptly, and into the sudden, sharp silence—)*

HUNTER. It's being yourself.

BLACKOUT

ACT TWO

The scene is the same. The Act One signs have been removed or replaced. A large banner posted that reads: VICTORY DANCE FRIDAY — SCHOOL GYM! HUNTER is alone, Downstage Center, addressing the audience.

HUNTER. I've got it all. I mean—I really do have it all. Big house. Great car. Plenty of bucks. And more where that came from. Not that the old man was always loaded. I've seen pictures of when I was small—the three bedroom crackerbox in the ticky tacky suburb, not a tree for miles and all the streets were named Elm or Maple or Shady Lane. Man, it's weird to look at those pictures. The old lady doesn't have her year-round tan, the old man doesn't have his briefcase. *(Softer, even sadly, remembering)* And the pictures of them together—those are the weirdest of all. . . .*(Quickly)* Of course I understand all about why the old man split. He explained it to me. My Dad and I never talked much—when you're raking in the bucks you don't want some snotty, stupid kid hanging on you. I mean, we *talked*—father and son stuff. *(And now his voice becomes louder—and louder, the tempo increasingly frantic, as his anger slips out)* You know—"How 'bout them Hawks?" or "How 'bout them Giants? Or Knicks? Or Jays? Or Bulls or Bears? *(At fever pitch)* Or Reds or Blues or Mets or Jets—" *(He stops short, pulling himself together)* And when I got a little overheated with that one chick, he

50

told me to cool it, because it can cost a guy a bundle if he
gets a broad knocked up. But when he left, we had a real
man-to-man. He said he'd found this girl—that she
made him feel young. *(He's trying hard)* I can understand
that. Everyone wants to be young, right? Mom tries to be
young. *(The anger returning, his volume increasing with his pace,
as he loses control)* She's always playing tennis or at her
aerobics class—always getting her legs waxed or her
tummy tucked or her saddlebags suctioned— *(At fever
pitch)* Always getting her hair tinted or dyed or permed or
her face tightened or peeled or painted— *(He stops short,
collecting himself)* I think she had a face lift once. She didn't
say anything, but she went away for about a week, and
when she came home, she wore these dark glasses
around everywhere. When she finally took 'em off, I'd
always catch her looking in the mirror, muttering things
like, "That'll get him". She knows a lot of people, at her
club—in her dumped wives support group. Oh, that's
not what they call it, but that's what it is. And then there's
her best friends. The little white ones, the little pink ones,
the little blue ones. . . . Yeah, she's got a whole medicine
cabinet full of friends. I came home real late one night,
and she was singing and laughing, real up—real happy.
(Happy himself) I thought—Dad's coming back! *(His eager-
ness fades)* But she'd just met her first friend. . . . She
explained it all to me. She said a woman can't drink, you
get fat if you drink and ruin your skin. Pills just make the
pain go away. *(Bitterly)* And she was right. They're the ˙
best friends of all. Better than friends. Better than
parents. They're always there when you need 'em—and
they never let you down. *(HUNTER slams out Down Left,*

*SHARON, BARB and PAT at their lockers, as BROOKE enters
the lounge Right, the others very deliberately ignoring her)*

BROOKE. *(Defiantly, yet near tears)* I suppose we're off for
the mall? Again.

SHARON. *(Carelessly, not even looking at her)* I suppose.
(Trying to force a confrontation, BROOKE moves closer)

BROOKE. And the party? What about that?

BARB. *(Briefly)* Got me.

BROOKE. All right. It's finally getting through—you
don't have to waste anymore time snubbing me. *(The three
gather up their books, crossing Left, as BROOKE calls after them)*
I'd just like to know why, that's all—why you're doing
it— *(Her voice breaks. As the other two exit, PAT hangs back)*

PAT. *(Bluntly)* You should have given Hunt what he
wanted when he wanted it.

BROOKE. *(Understanding)* *He* did this—he told everyone
to dump me—

PAT. *(With a shrug, hard)* Dump—or be dumped.

BROOKE. And I suppose he thinks now I'll be willing to
do anything to get back in!

PAT. I would. *(Then bitterly)* I did.

BROOKE. *(Almost to herself)* I thought you and the other
girls were so secure—so sure of yourselves—but you're
just as worried about being out of it as I was—

PAT. *(Shrewdly, catching her)* It doesn't matter to you
anymore?

BROOKE. *(She can barely say it)* It matters.

PAT. Then you'd better make real sure Scott Barrows
shows up at the dance Friday night.

BROOKE. *(Protesting, hedging)* I don't even know him—
we've only talked a couple of times—

PAT. He's always looking at you! *(Sarcastically)* You're the girl of his dreams! If he hadn't been defending what he thought was your honor, Hunt would never have been expelled. *(BROOKE looks at her, PAT unblinking, as the bell rings, the lounge filling with students. Over the noise, we hear Pat and Brooke's dialogue)* So what about it—can we count on you?

BROOKE. *(Briefly)* You can count on me.

PAT. *(Smiling)* I thought so. *(PAT and Brooke exit the lounge Right and Left, above the din rises the dreadful, deadly cheeriness of the announcement voice)*

ANNOUNCEMENT VOICE. Good morning everyone! *(The usual cattle call of sounds answer her)* And here are today's announcements: *(Picking up tempo as she goes)* Debate club has been moved to the drama room—drama to the art room—art to the choir room—choir to the orchestra room—orchestra to the band room— *(And this is the part she's been waiting for, with sadistic joy)* thereby leaving the band with absolutely no place at all!! Today's hot lunch is: Mystery Meat and Maalox casserole, and Roadside Surprise—consisting of anything the food service manager ran over this morning! *(And then, above the hoots, the whistles, the laughter, she screams out, totally losing it)* Someone has tampered with my hot lunch!!

BUZZARD. *(Calling out)* What's the big deal?

LEN. The man just added a few gourmet touches! *(As the lounge clears, BURNOUT and LEN cross Downstage Right and Left, BUZZARD forming the apex of the triangle Upstage, for a three part monologue addressed to the audience)*

BUZZARD. I suppose this means detention again—

LEN. —again—

BURNOUT. —again.

BUZZARD. It's not that I like getting in trouble—

LEN. Speak for yourself.

BUZZARD. *(Loftily)* I just march to the beat of a different drummer.

BURNOUT. In whose band?

BUZZARD. My band! My beat! *(Distinctly)* The beat of a different drummer. I read that once somewhere. I even wrote it down. I like to look at it when I'm gettin' flak.

BURNOUT. Which is always.

BUZZARD. *(Flatly)* Which is always.

LEN. Some guys see things straight as an arrow. Black and white. Good and bad.

BURNOUT. I remember back at summer camp, all the kids hated the food—but I was the only one who did anything constructive about it.

BUZZARD. She started a food fight.

LEN. I see things all crooked—and tangled up.

BURNOUT. Then in Biology, I was the one who freed all the worms and let the crayfish go.

BUZZARD. Don't they have rights?

BURNOUT. I flunked my personality test. The school told my parents I didn't have one. I think what they meant was, I didn't have *theirs.*

LEN. Sometimes I don't see things at all.

BUZZARD. *(Wonderingly)* Carnelli said he didn't want to see my spirit broken.

BURNOUT. *(Wryly)* Is that what you call it?

BUZZARD. Now that I've found out what it is that I've got—I don't think I want to lose it. *(They exit the lounge, SYBIL and VINCE in the small playing area Left. SYBIL is an attractive woman, a tense edge beneath her sophisticated veneer)*

SYBIL. Hunt tells me you want him to apologize to this Ms. Healy before you'll let him back in school. Don't you think that's a little extreme?

VINCE. He shoved a teacher. He insulted her. Those seem like major items to me.

SYBIL. *(With polished, practiced cool)* Everyone knows what it's like in schools these days. This woman accepted the job—she should be willing to accept the problems as well.

VINCE. *(Bluntly)* That's a copout.

SYBIL. *(Patronizingly)* Mr. Carnelli, your salary is public record. You can't really expect Hunter to take orders from a man who doesn't earn in a year what his father gives away in tips?

VINCE. *(This doesn't faze him, he might even smile at her)* Where is Hunter's Father today? I asked to see both of you.

SYBIL. *(Quickly, defensively—covering)* Why? Do you want to order him around, too? Would that make you feel even more powerful?

VINCE. *(Patiently)* I'm not engaged in any power plays here. *(Calling her bluff)* And I think you know it.

SYBIL. *(Snapping it out)* Hunter's Father and I are divorced.

VINCE. From each other—not from your son.

SYBIL. *(Pointedly evading the issue)* I'm seriously considering sending Hunt to a prep school out East. What do you think of that?

VINCE. *(Just as pointed)* I think it's time you stopped allowing your son to run away from his problems. *(Distinctly)* Hunter needs help.

SYBIL. *(Almost desperately)* You've got to understand, Mr. Carnelli—it hasn't been easy for Hunt. *(And this isn't easy for her)* About his Father—It's not—he doesn't— *(Carefully, distinctly)* Hunter doesn't really have a father.

CARNELLI. *(Bluntly)* He's got a mother, doesn't he? *(Quickly, angrily, with a small sound of outrage, SYBIL stands, they look at one another, then—)*

SYBIL. *(Shorn of pretense)* He used to have one. *(SYBIL turns sharply and exits, crossing Downstage. Lights cross fade to spot)* I haven't been a mother for a long time. I haven't been anything for a long time. I haven't wanted to *be* anything! Especially not who I am. *(Bursting out with it)* So I take some pills! More than I used to. More than I should. What's wrong with that? And what's wrong with wanting to run away from things? Everybody's running away from something! Mostly from themselves. . . . *(Desperately)* What's wrong with wanting to just drift—to just feel good? Even for a little while. . . . I don't even know if Hunt would listen to me anymore—I don't even know if there's anything left inside me to say. Maybe just . . . don't be like me. *(Lights up. She exits Downstage, BROOKE at her locker, as SCOTT enters Left. He's eager, he's awkward, he's hesitant—he's hopeful)*

SCOTT. Brooke!— *(She turns quickly, almost as if stunned at the sight of him)* Hello—

BROOKE. *(Unable to meet his eyes)* Hi, Scott—

SCOTT. *(With vaulting enthusiasm)* Hi! That is— *(Finishing flatly, lamely)* Hi. *(She hurries quickly away from him, head down, unaware even of what she's saying)*

BROOKE. See ya—

SCOTT. *(Seeing her going, he bursts out with it)* The dance—

(She stops, he gathers up his courage) Do you want to go to the dance with me?

BROOKE. *(Slowly, as she turns back to him)* You want to go—with me?

SCOTT. *(Is she kidding?)* I want to go anywhere with you! If you don't want to go to the dance, we can go someplace else—anyplace! You name it!

BROOKE. *(Hating herself)* The dance is fine.

SCOTT. *(Almost dithering)* This—this is great! More than great! *(At a loss, in his excitement, for what to say next)* Uh—I— I'll pick you up! That's it! I'll pick you up—Friday! Night!

BROOKE. *(Smiling, almost sadly)* You don't have a car.

SCOTT. Minor problem! *(Crossing backwards Right)* I'll borrow one! I'll buy one! I'll steal one!

BROOKE. *(Quickly, as if pleading)* Scott, don't—

SCOTT. What?

BROOKE. *(But she can't say it)* Don't go to too much trouble. . . . *(As BROOKE and SCOTT exit the lounge Left and Right, JEN, HOWIE, MONICA, and ALEX take their original Downstage positions from Act One, the first three again anxious, increasingly frantic, ALEX cool and confident, the dialogue slap sharp, nearly overlapping)*

JEN. The dance—

HOWIE. The dance—

MONICA. The dance—

ALEX. The dance!

HOWIE. No date—

MONICA. Did he really ask me?—

JEN. No date—

MONICA. Why'd he ask me?—

ALEX. Two dates!

HOWIE. It'll be dumb!—

MONICA. I'll look weird!

JEN. It'll be a disaster!—

HOWIE. I'll look gross!

MONICA. It'll be depressing!—

JEN. I'll look desperate!

HOWIE, MONICA, JEN. I am desperate!—

MONICA. What if he doesn't show?

ALEX. This could be my lucky night! *(An abrupt pause, then into the silence, we hear his doubt)* I hope—

OFFSTAGE VOICE. What time is the—

HOWIE, MONICA, JEN, ALEX. *(In varying degrees of panic and hope)* dance! *(The four exit Downstage, ED, BEV, and CORLY at the Barrows table Right, SCOTT entering—but this time he slides happily into his chair, a large silly smile on his face as he regards them all fondly)*

SCOTT. Hi! *(In unison, they stop and stare at him, forks midway to open mouths, instantly suspicious, SCOTT digging into dinner)*

ED. What's wrong?

SCOTT. Nothing's wrong!

ED. You're smiling.

BEV. You're eating!

CORLY. *(Totally disgusted)* You're happy.

SCOTT. I've got a date for the dance tonight.

BEV. That's nice, dear.

SCOTT. Nice?! *(What's wrong with the woman)* It's better than nice—it's better than wonderful—it's better than fantastic—

CORLY. *(Complacently)* I knew this would happen.

SCOTT. *(In disbelief)* You did?

CORLY. *(Sweetly)* It was only a matter of time until you slipped over the edge.

ED. *(Dryly)* Good for you, Bachelor No. One.

CORLY. *(Suspiciously)* Did the Father just make a joke?

BEV. Yes, dear.

CORLY. At his age you can never tell if it's humor—or senility. *(And CORLY gets two simultaneous "looks" from ED and BEV)*

ED. But now I want your decision, Scott. About college. *(Dryly)* You do remember college? The place you go so you don't have to work with your hands.

BEV. *(With a complacency to match Corley's)* Scott *is* going to work with his hands. He's going to be an artist.

SCOTT. *(In amazement)* You know?

BEV. *(Dryly)* You learn a lot about a person when you clean his room for 17 years.

ED. *(Trying to fathom this)* You mean, you want to go to New York, dress weird—live with roaches?

CORLY. Please—I'm eating.

SCOTT. *(Tentatively)* I mean—I want to go to art school.

ED. He's crazy! *This* is crazy!

BEV. *(Mildly—yet with a firm edge)* Maybe so, Ed, but I've lived half my life and there's only one thing I know for sure—life is supposed to be crazy. So you might as well sit back and enjoy it.

ED. *(Pleading his case)* I wanted college for you, Scott—I wanted you to make something of yourself!

SCOTT. *(Fighting back)* You never finished college and

you made something of yourself.

ED. Not enough!

BEV. Enough for us.

ED. *(Painfully)* Not enough for me.

BEV. *(Gently)* This isn't about you, Ed. You said it yourself—it's Scott's turn now.

ED. *(This is difficult)* This art thing—it's what you really want?

SCOTT. Yes, Dad.

ED. And it makes you happy?

SCOTT. Yes, Dad.

ED. *(Struggling)* Then—do it.

SCOTT. *(A wealth of meaning in his few words as well)* Thanks, Dad.

CORLY. This is starting to sound like a sensitive greeting card.

ED. *(Pondering this)* A painter, huh? Maybe you could paint the garage this summer.

SCOTT. *(Smiling)* Sure thing, Dad. *(He stands)* Gotta get ready for the dance—

BEV. Just a few more carrots—*(But he's gone)*

CORLY. *(Indicating the carrots, distastefully)* Frozen, I suppose?

BEV. *(With a tight lipped smile)* Piggly Wiggly's best.

CORLY. *(With that irritating rightness)* Actually, organically grown, naturally fertilized vegetables provide the only real source of authentic protein.

BEV. *(She's definitely had it)* Then you grow them—and mulch them—and especially fertilize them! *(Standing, she leans right in to the open-mouthed Corly, enjoying every distinct word of this)* I'm going out for a marshmallow and hot

fudge sundae—filled with preservatives—heaped with
calories—loaded with carbohydrates—laden with cholesterol—and topped with nuts!! *(As if summoning him to
battle)* Ed—are you with me?! *(And ED quickly hops to)*

CORLY. *(In horror)* Don't you realize you may be rotting
out what few natural teeth you have left—not to mention
embarking on a white sugar high from which there may
be no return?!

BEV, ED. Yes!! *(And triumphantly, defiantly, they exit)*

CORLY. *(In total disbelief)* Art school. Chocolate. *Happiness.* What do they think this is—the sixties?! *(KARL and
LIBBY enter the lounge Left, dressed for the dance. LIBBY is
shaken, rather wobbly, KARL awkwardly aiding her)*

LIBBY. *(Angry at herself and humiliation)* I was so sick—
sick and dizzy. Like I had the flu. *(She sits)* Now I just feel
stupid. *(Turning from him)* Throwing up in the parking
lot—

KARL. Where'd you get the booze?

LIBBY. Pat asked me to her house—there were a bunch
of other kids there. They gave me a few beers and then
some hard stuff. Everything was pretty much of a blur
until I got to the gym. When I started dancing, the room
started spinning. *(Almost reaching for his comfort)* If you
hadn't taken me outside—if one of the teachers had
seen—

KARL. It's okay now. *(BARB, SHARON and PAT enter
Right, a little giggly, very up)*

PAT. *(Knowingly, looking from Karl to Libby)* So how's it
going?

LIBBY. *(Embarrassed)* All right.

SHARON. *(With meaning)* Just all right?!

PAT. You were hangin' real loose last time we looked, Libby. *(There's a burst of laughter at this, LIBBY wincing, laughter punctuating the rest of the comments by the three)*

BARB. Did anything happen in the parking lot we should know about?

PAT. Did you get it on?

KARL. *(Tersely)* Beat it.

SHARON. Maybe they want some privacy—

BARB. Maybe they're gonna get it on now!—

SHARON. Can we watch?!

PAT. How about it, Libby? Need another six pack to get you started?

KARL. *(Lashing out)* You couldn't leave her alone, could you? You couldn't just let her stay the way she was!

PAT. *(Hard)* All we did was show her how to get mellow—if she can't handle it, that's her problem. *(The three exit, maybe muttering a few comments as they go, stifling laughter)*

KARL. *(At a loss)* Why'd you do it?

LIBBY. *(Defiantly)* Why not? *(She stands)* Take a few drinks and suddenly you're bright and funny, all sparkly and shiny—right? *(Bitterly)* and even if you're not—you don't care.

KARL. You don't need booze to be those things.

LIBBY. I need something! Why did I do it? So I wouldn't be me—just for a little while. So I wouldn't be so uptight! So I could talk and dance and laugh and *be* those other girls! *(A pause, then simply)* So you'd like me.

KARL. I do like you!

LIBBY. *(With painful sarcasm)* Well, thanks. In spite of

everything—you like me.

KARL. *(Earnestly)* You've got it all wrong, don't you know that? Not *in spite of—because of!*

LIBBY. *(She looks at him, then, wonderingly—)* Somebody told me once that I was too quiet—too different—for anyone ever to notice me. For the first time . . . I think he might have been wrong. *(They exit the lounge Right, hand in hand, as JEN and MONICA enter Downstage Right and Left, staying on opposite sides of the stage to address the audience in a point/counterpoint dialogue without self pity, only the bright bite of pain and broken dreams. They're dressed for the dance)*

MONICA. He was so popular—and good looking. A jock.

JEN. A hunk, really.

MONICA. And he asked *me* to the dance!

JEN. And there he was—smiling at *me* across the gym!

MONICA. It was like a dream—

JEN. Like a short story in *True Romance.*

MONICA. Mom said she'd always known that someday someone would come along who'd appreciate my finer qualities. I really thought someone had. . . .

JEN. So *I* smiled back!

MONICA. I bought a new dress. Had my hair done. Bought some make-up—the kind they advertise on TV, especially for teenagers with sensitive skin. I put on the dress. Combed out my hair. Put on the base and the blush and the pencil and the shadow and the lipstick— *cherry kiss*—and waited.

JEN. And *he* smiled back!

MONICA. I wiped off the lipstick and put on some

more. Redid my hair. Sprayed perfume on the backs of my knees, just like the magazines say. And I waited.

JEN. And *I* smiled—and tossed my head and flipped my hair. All at the same time! I felt like Cheryl Tiegs!

MONICA. Dad went upstairs. Mom started crying. And then I knew.

JEN. And then he started walking towards me—

MONICA. Or maybe I'd always known.

JEN. —and kept right on walking—

MONICA. He wasn't going to show. It was all a joke. I'd been set up. Again.

JEN. —and asked the girl behind me to dance.

MONICA. The prince wasn't going to come knocking at my door.

JEN. So I turned to my friends and kept on pretending I was having a good time. *(PAT enters Upstage, to form the apex of the triangle. She, too, is without self-pity, only hard acceptance, as she addresses the audience)*

PAT. I was late last month. I was really sweatin' it for a couple of days. But it turned out to be a false alarm. So I'm safe. Until the next time. I know some of the kids think I'm a tramp—and maybe I am. I only know that as scared as I was those days I thought I was in trouble—I'm more scared of being alone. . . . *(JEN and MONICA exit Down Right and Left, PAT exiting Upstage, as ALEX and TRAVIS shove Scott into the lounge Right. They've got his arms pinned behind him, SCOTT struggling against them)*

SCOTT. I hope this makes you guys feel real tough— two against one.

TRAVIS. *(Without humor)* Those are my kinds of odds.

HUNTER. *(Coolly, entering Left)* Mr. Barrows—so glad

you could make it. We've got a lot to settle.

SCOTT. Then why don't we? Settle it, I mean. Just the two of us. One on one.

HUNTER. *(Patronizingly)* Broken beer bottles at 50 paces? Arm wrestling? That may be the way the lower classes handle things, but it's not my style.

SCOTT. I didn't figure it was. You haven't got the guts to fight it out alone.

HUNTER. *(Angrily)* And you haven't got the brains to shut up and beg for mercy! Take him outside and introduce him to the rest of our friends.

TRAVIS. *(Twisting Scott's arm sharply, the pain showing)* The odds are going to get even better out there, buddy. *(As ALEX and TRAVIS attempt to hustle Scott out Left, LEN, BURN-OUT, HOWIE and BROOKE enter Left. They're visibly nervous, but determined, ready for a confrontation, BUZZARD trailing)*

HOWIE. *(Jittery but firm)* We're here to help Scott!

TRAVIS. I thought the misfits of science were having a convention.

BROOKE. Hunter used me to set you up, Scott—I didn't have the nerve to tell you—

LEN. However—she did tell us.

HUNTER. *(To Brooke, viciously)* So you're the one who hustled up all the geeks. What did you do—raid a sideshow?

BURNOUT. Let him go!

ALEX. Or what? You'll hit us with your hair spray can?

TRAVIS. *(This is to Howie)* Or maybe your computer paper?

LEN. I could point out that there are more of us than there are of you.

ALEX. Yeah, but all our parts are working.

BROOKE. *(Turning)* I'm going to get Carnelli—

HUNTER. *(Grabbing her, brutally)* Do it—and you're dead at this school!

BROOKE. *(Pulling sharply away)* I don't think I care anymore. *(She runs out Right)*

HUNTER. *(Enraged)* Forget her! We'll be done by the time she gets back! *(Indicating Left)* Waste him!

HOWIE. *(He shoves himself forward, pushing up his glasses with a nervous gesture)* You'll have to go through us first. *(And LEN and BURNOUT go shoulder to shoulder with Howie)*

LEN. Trite—but true.

TRAVIS. That ought to take all of 30 seconds.

KARL. *(Entering Right, with purpose, LIBBY behind him)* I'd give it a little longer.

HUNTER. Butt out, Swanson—this isn't your fight.

KARL. *(With bitter memory)* Oh, yes it is. Guys like you— they're always beatin' on people too little or too scared or too outnumbered to fight back. Yeah, I know all about guys like you. But why? Why do you do it? That's what I can't figure. Does tearin' down someone else make you feel bigger or better or stronger? Is that it?

HUNTER. *(Viciously)* You don't know what you're talking about—you're just a dump, stupid jock!

LIBBY. Don't listen to him, Karl—

HUNTER. *(Closing in for the kill)* You can't even play football anymore, your knees are so shot. So you're going to have an operation—big deal, they never work. You'll never play again—and then you won't even be a jock. *(Deliberately)* You'll just be a dumb—stupid—zero.

LIBBY. *(Pleading with him)* You don't need football to be someone, Karl—I didn't need liquor and you don't need football. You already are somebody! No matter what happens—you'll always be the same person inside!

KARL. *(Quietly)* Whatever I am—or maybe it's whatever I'm *not*—I know this isn't fair. *(Right to Alex and Travis, with clenched fist meaning)* Let him go.

BUZZARD. *(Suddenly, shouldering forward, with level determination)* Just a minute, Karl—you're not keeping me out of this one. No one's keeping me outta this one. I coulda never done this before—I been stuck inside my own head since I got to this school. But now I got a few things figured out. *(Indicating his friends)* These guys are my buddies—we've done time in deten together—and you can sure learn a lot in deten. We and my buddies—we look different from each other. Maybe we even think different. But we're not. Different. We're the same. *(Really moving in on the other three)* And you know what, Mr. Cool Guys? We're the same, too. That's right. *(To Alex, Travis and Hunter in turn)* Me and you—and me and you—and me and you— *(Indicating the two groups)* And *you* and *us*—we're the same. Oh, not where it shows—but where it counts. Deep down. In our guts. and you know it, too. That's what's got you so mad—and so scared. You know it, too. So take me outside—beat me to a pulp—use my head for a roto rooter. Even if I lose, I win. 'Cuz I got it all figured out. *(There's a pause, BUZZARD going eyeball to eyeball with them, and then TRAVIS backs off)*

TRAVIS. *(Wryly)* Maybe tonight the cards are all stacked

your way.

HUNTER. *(Enraged)* You can't just walk out on me!

TRAVIS. *(Very off hand)* Sure I can. See, I only hang around with important guys, and you know what, Hunt? You're not important anymore. *(And he exits Left)*

HUNTER. *(Demanding—almost pleading)* Alex!—

ALEX. *(Hesitating, then)* Sorry— *(ALEX takes off after Travis, as the others high five it in celebration. Struggling to save face, HUNTER casts a glance around the group, cool battling rage and humiliation)*

HUNTER. Everything he said was a bunch of crap— you're still losers! *(HUNTER crashes out of the scene and Downstage to spot—The others freeze. He addresses the audience with bravado)*

HUNTER. I don't care—about them, about anyone. About anything. Why should I? I've got it all. The house. The wheels. The bucks. *(A pause, then bitterly)* And all my friends. . . . *(He pulls a vial of pills from his pocket, and with an emphatic gesture, tosses down a couple, then quickly exits Downstage)*

HOWIE. *(In disbelief)* We did it!

BUZZARD. *The Magnificent Seven* ride again!

HOWIE. *(Weakly)* I think I'm going to faint—

BUZZARD. *(Flatly)* Maybe not exactly the *magnificent seven*— *(COZLOWE and CARNELLI enter Right, BROOKE with them)*

VINCE. What's the trouble here?

SCOTT. *(Quickly)* No trouble.

COZLOWE. *(With grim satisfaction)* Well, then—loitering is against the rules. *(Muttering and casting a few well chosen looks, LEN, BURNOUT and even HOWIE, exit Right)*

BUZZARD. *(With new zeal)* But free assembly is a constitutional right! You could look it up—in my report. *(Too off hand)* You know, the one in the blue folder with my address clearly marked on the cover. *(Really laying it on)* And all those *great—straight—*lines.

COZLOWE. *(Dryly)* I seem to recall it.

BUZZARD. *(Loftly)* Wait until you hear my original ideas regarding the causes and effects of the Revolutionary War not commonly found in most major American textbooks!

COZLOWE. *(Emphatically)* I have a rule against opinions in my classes. *(And she exits Right)*

BUZZARD. *(Calling after her)* The Constitution guarantees our right to free speech! You could look it up! *(Back to the others, with a grin)* This could be the beginning of a beautiful friendship! *(And he hustles after her, Right)*

KARL. *(With difficulty)* Mr. Carnelli, you said I gotta open up. Start talkin' about—things. I think I'm ready now.

VINCE. If you need someone to listen, I'm available.

LIBBY. *(Warmly)* He has someone.

KARL. *(A smile for Libby, then—)* I just want you to know, no matter how things turn out, there's gonna be somethin' for me—after.

VINCE. I never doubted it. *(LIBBY, KARL and VINCE exit Right, SCOTT and BROOKE awkwardly facing one another)*

SCOTT. Thanks—

BROOKE. *(Sharply)* I don't deserve that.

SCOTT. *(Wryly)* Maybe we could *finish* the dance together.

BROOKE. You don't want me! *(Quickly she crosses to her locker, pulls out Seventeen, and tears off the cover, handing it to him)*

BROOKE. *(With force)* You want *her!* I tried to make myself over—change myself—turn myself into her! Or as close to her as I could get. And it worked! Everyone noticed me. *(Puzzling this out)* Only—only it was somebody made-up they were noticing. Somebody that doesn't even exist. Not me. I'm not even sure there *is* a me—

SCOTT. There is.

BROOKE. *(Bursting out with it)* But that's what I'm afraid of! What if me really is boring—what if she can't measure up—can't figure out where's she's going—or why—

SCOTT. You've still got to take the chance. *(And firmly, with a single stroke, he tears the cover in two. A bell rings, the lounge filling with students and the noisy hum of conversation and laughter. ED, BEV, and CORLY are Right, ED reading the Wall Street Journal, CORLY reading a high fiber, high protein cereal box, BEV chowing down a hot fudge sundae. VINCE is in his office, COZLOWE in the lounge with a student, HEALY also, or she can double as a student, SYBIL down Right, apart. They don't step out of place to address the audience, sometimes just turning their heads to shout over their shoulder, as the sound of the school— of life itself—continues unabated around them)*

HOWIE. Acne!

SHARON. Asthma!

JEN. Bod?!

ALEX. Blotches!

VINCE. I came here to help kids. I think I can make a difference. But can anyone really be sure?

BARB. *(Indicating her hair)* Home perm!

JEN. *(Indicating her clothes)* Home made!

TRAVIS. Home!!

PAT. Sometimes I get so tired of all the flak.

BURNOUT. Sometimes I just get tired.

LEN. And confused.

HOWIE. Real confused.

LIBBY. I ask for an explanation—

BURNOUT. But no one's got one that I can understand.

KARL. Or no one's got one at all.

SYBIL. I know what I should do.

HUNTER. Dump the pills.

SYBIL. Talk to my son. To myself. And I will. Tomorrow. Or the next day . . .

HUNTER. Today.

SYBIL. We'll start over. Start again. Find our way—

HUNTER. Out.

SYBIL. Back.

MONICA. The night of the dance I wanted to die. I really, really wanted to die. But in the morning I was all right. Well, maybe not all right—but better. Maybe not even better. But okay. You see, there really is something wonderful about me. Maybe it's hidden now, way down deep. Maybe I'm the only one who knows it's there—but I'm the only one who has to.

ALEX. Overwhelmed!

LEN. Outnumbered!

HOWIE. Out of it!

MONICA. Okay!

THE OTHERS. Okay!

JEN. Maybe there's a few of us who really do have it

all together.

LIBBY. And the rest of us?

PAT. We're just trying to survive.

HUNTER. Just—trying.

BROOKE. Waiting to see how we'll turn out.

BUZZARD. So what do you think our chances are?

SCOTT. I think we're going to make it.

END